Welcome to a Tale of Asgard...

Thor, the prince of Asgard, is a brash and impetuous youth. Never one to consider who he is or what he has, Thor's mind is always on who he will one day be and what the future holds for him. He feels he lives in the shadow of his father, Odin, ruler of all Asgard, and he hopes he can escape that fate through noble deeds and valiant acts.

After sneaking into the imperial armory and attempting to lift the mighty uru hammer, Mjolnir, Thor and his warrior friends, Balder and Sif, are attacked by three monstrous spiders, set loose on the trio by Thor's jealous half-brother Loki. Working as a team, the trio defeats their arachnid foes. Fearing punishment for their actions, the teens are surprised to win praise from Odin himself for their heroics in battle. Having now proven themselves accomplished warriors, Odin asks the valiant youths to undertake a quest on his behalf: they must travel Asgard in search of four mystic elements that he will use to forge an enchanted sword. Without consulting Balder or Sif, Thor accepts the quest on their behalf, which does not sit well with the young warriors.

Their first task leads them to Nastrond, in search of the dragon Hakurei, from whose hide the young heroes are meant to pluck a scale. Much to their surprise, the white dragon lies in wait, having been tipped off to their plan. After a vicious battle, the teen trio ultimately defeats Hakurei and escapes with one of the requested scales, but not without further damaging the group's already fragile morale.

Now, the disgruntled youths travel north to the snowy mountains of Jotunheim, where they must pluck a feather from the wing of the snow eagle, Gnori.

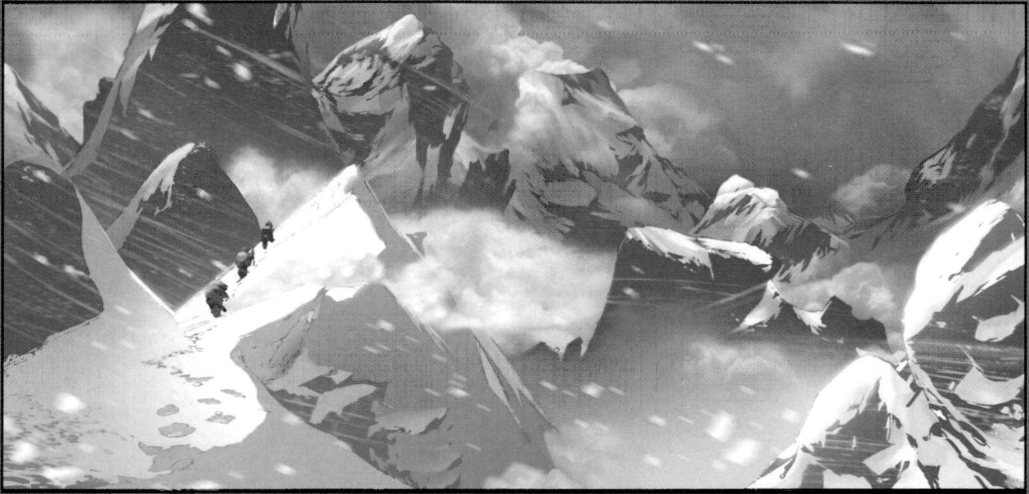

Part Three

The Nest of Gnori

Akira Yoshida
Writer

Greg Tocchini
Penciler

Jay Leisten
Inker

Guru eFX
Colorist

VC's Randy Gentile
Letterer

Adi Granov
Cover Artist

MacKenzie Cadenhead
Editor

Ralph Macchio & C.B. Cebulski
Consulting Editors

Joe Quesada
Editor in Chief

Dan Buckley
Publisher

MARVEL
Spotlight

VISIT US AT
www.abdopublishing.com

Reinforced library bound edition published in 2007 by Spotlight, a division of the ABDO Publishing Group, Edina, Minnesota. Spotlight produces high quality reinforced library bound editions for schools and libraries. Published by agreement with Marvel Characters, Inc.

Library of Congress Cataloging-in-Publication Data

Yoshida, Akira.
Thor, son of Asgard / [Akira Yoshida, writer ; Greg Tocchini, penciler ; Jay Leisten, inker ; Guru e FX, colorist ; Adi Granov, cover artist ; Randy Gentile, letterer].
p. cm.
Cover title.
"Marvel Age."
Revisions of issues 1-6 of the serial Thor, son of Asgard.
Contents: pt. 1. The warriors teen -- pt. 2. The heat of Hakurei -- pt. 3. The nest of Gnori -- pt. 4. The jaws of Jennia -- pt. 5. The lake of Lilitha -- pt. 6. The trio triumphant.
ISBN-13: 978-1-59961-286-7 (pt. 1)
ISBN-10: 1-59961-286-0 (pt. 1)
ISBN-13: 978-1-59961-287-4 (pt. 2)
ISBN-10: 1-59961-287-9 (pt. 2)
ISBN-13: 978-1-59961-288-1 (pt. 3)
ISBN-10: 1-59961-288-7 (pt. 3)
ISBN-13: 978-1-59961-289-8 (pt. 4)
ISBN-10: 1-59961-289-5 (pt. 4)
ISBN-13: 978-1-59961-290-4 (pt. 5)
ISBN-10: 1-59961-290-9 (pt. 5)
ISBN-13: 978-1-59961-291-1 (pt. 6)
ISBN-10: 1-59961-291-7 (pt. 6)
1. Comic books, strips, etc. I. Tocchini, Greg. II. Title. III. Title: Warriors teen. IV. Title: Heat of Hakurei. V. Title: Nest of Gnori. VI. Title: Jaws of Jennia. VII. Title: Lake of Lilitha. VIII. Title: Trio triumphant.

PN6728.T64Y68 2007
791.5'73--dc22

2006050635

All Spotlight books are reinforced library binding and manufactured in the United States of America.

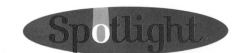

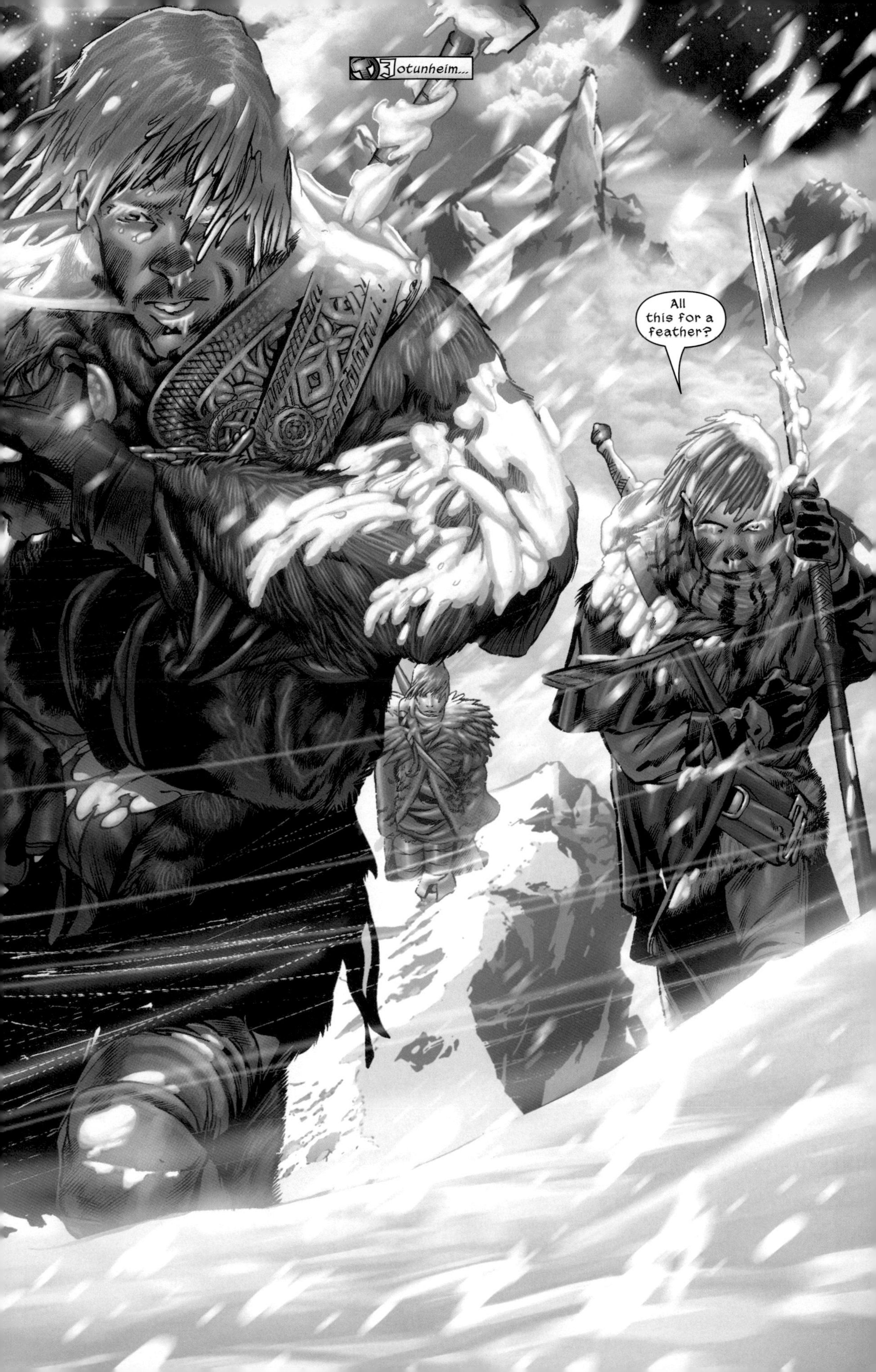
Jotunheim...
All this for a feather?

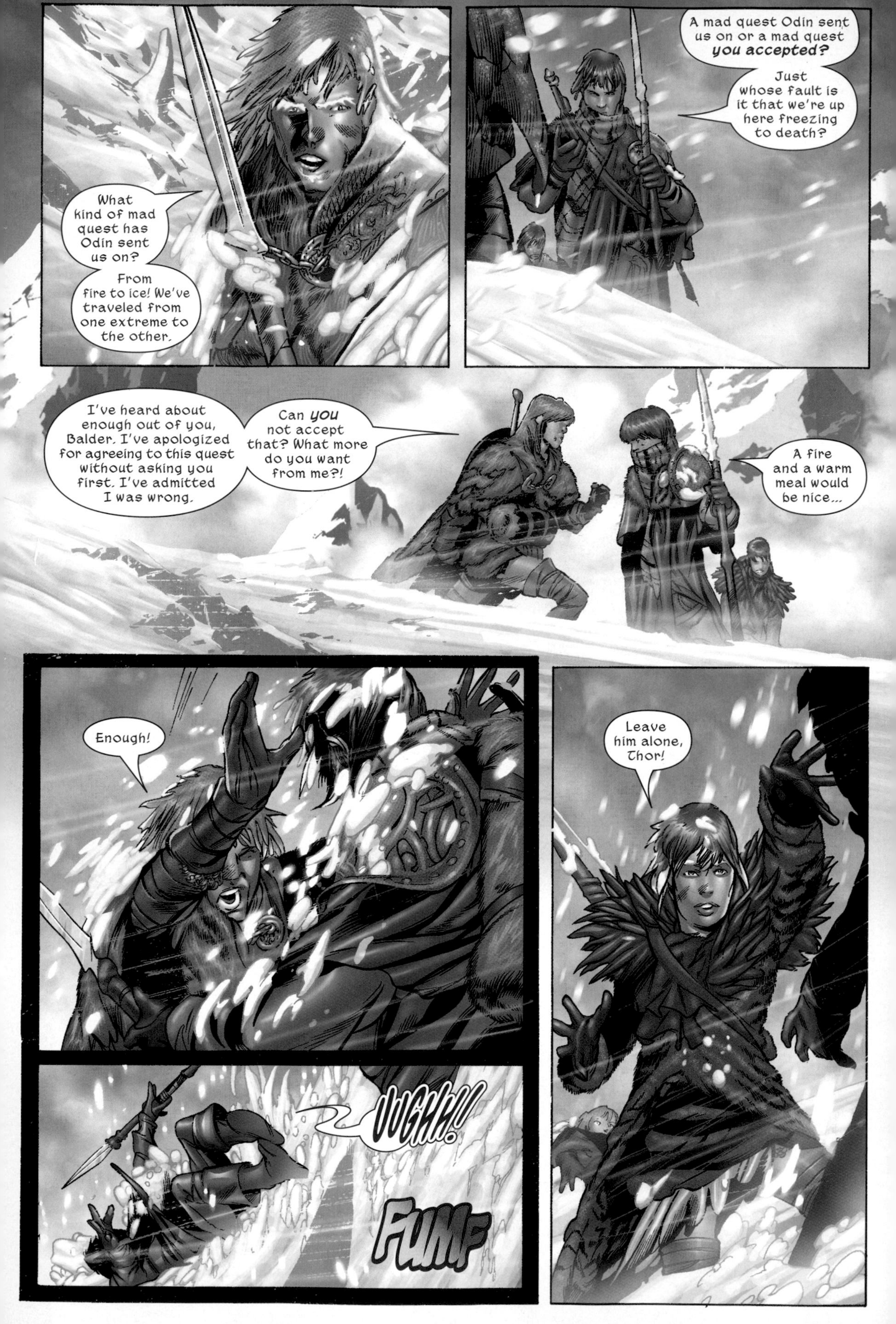

What kind of mad quest has Odin sent us on?
From fire to ice! We've traveled from one extreme to the other.
A mad quest Odin sent us on or a mad quest you accepted?
Just whose fault is it that we're up here freezing to death?
I've heard about enough out of you, Balder. I've apologized for agreeing to this quest without asking you first. I've admitted I was wrong.
Can you not accept that? What more do you want from me?!
A fire and a warm meal would be nice...
Enough!
UUGHH!!
FUMF
Leave him alone, Thor!

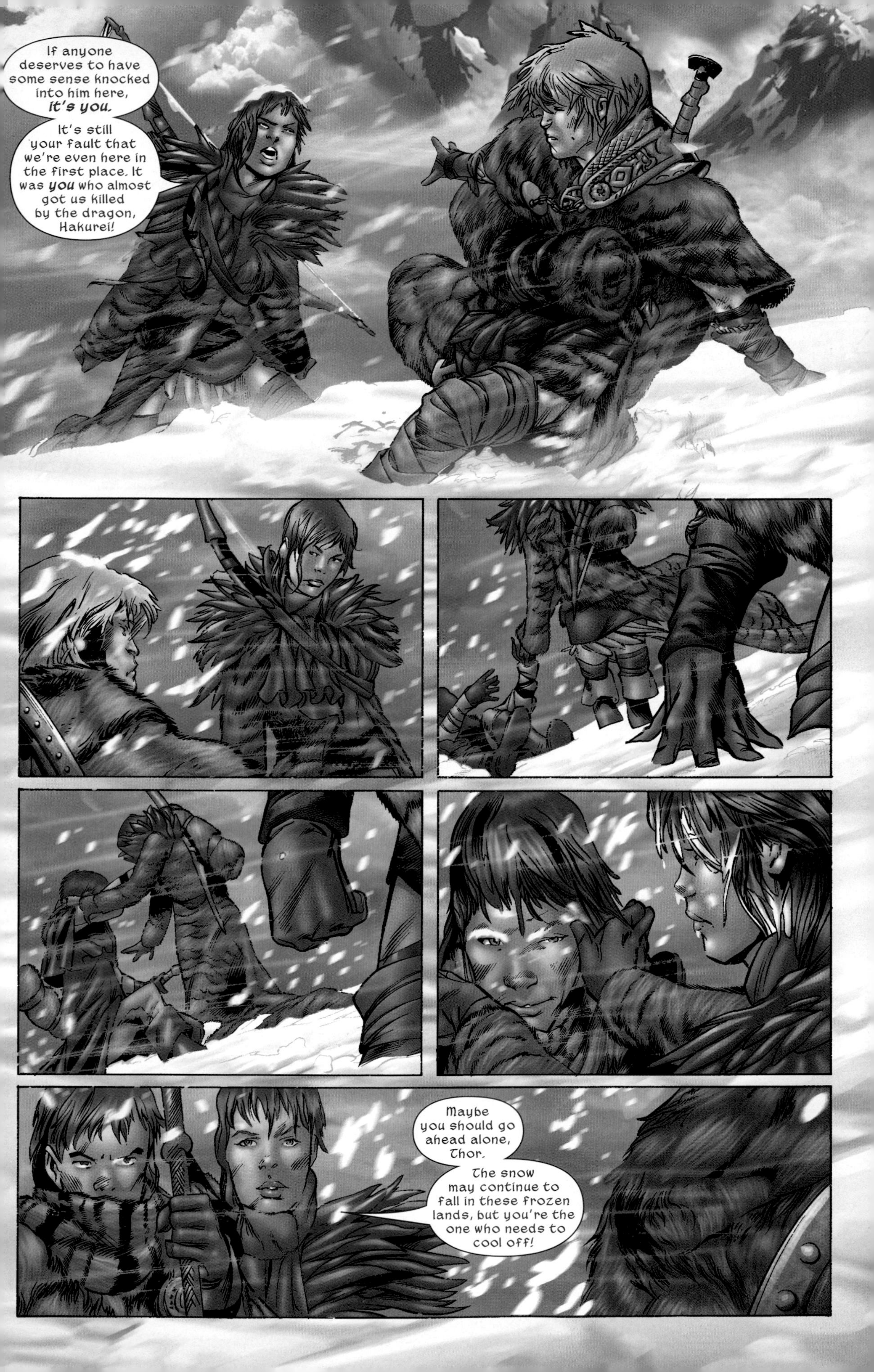
If anyone deserves to have some sense knocked into him here, *it's you.*
It's still your fault that we're even here in the first place. It was *you* who almost got us killed by the dragon, Hakurei!
Maybe you should go ahead alone, Thor.
The snow may continue to fall in these frozen lands, but you're the one who needs to cool off!

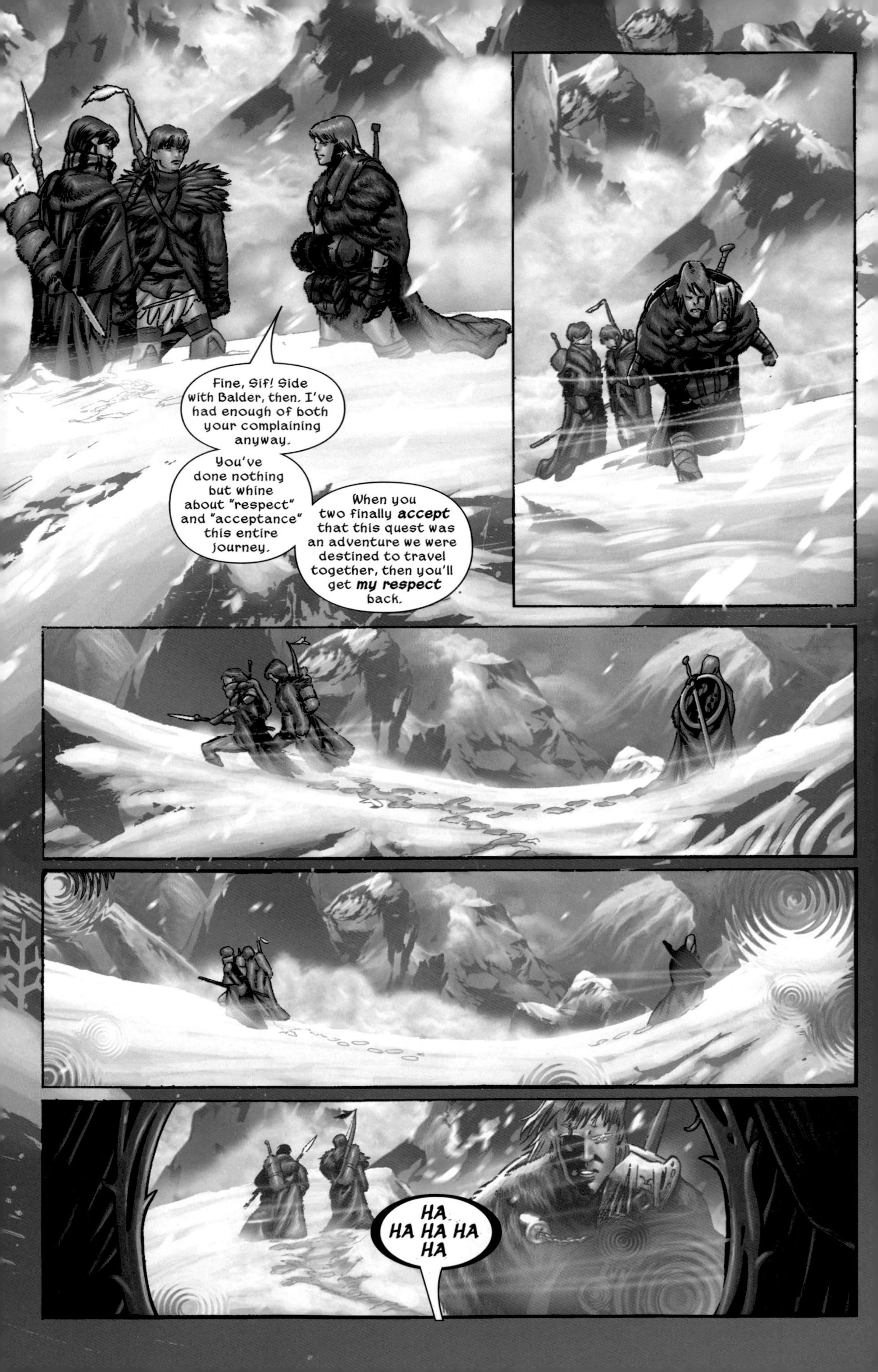
Fine, Sif! Side with Balder, then. I've had enough of both your complaining anyway.
You've done nothing but whine about "respect" and "acceptance" this entire journey.
When you two finally **accept** that this quest was an adventure we were destined to travel together, then you'll get ***my respect*** back.
HA HA HA HA HA

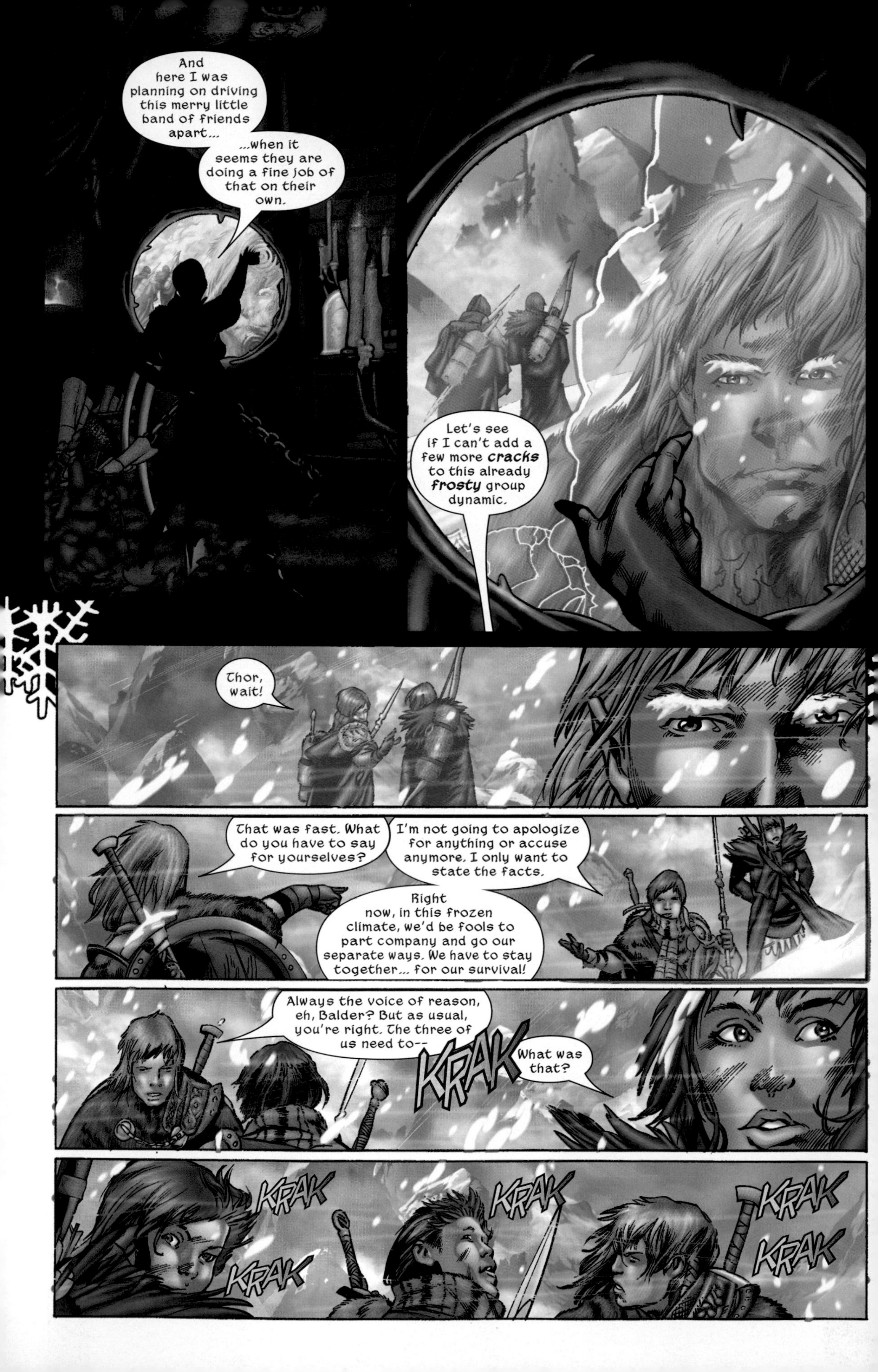

And here I was planning on driving this merry little band of friends apart...
...when it seems they are doing a fine job of that on their own.
Let's see if I can't add a few more cracks to this already frosty group dynamic.
Thor, wait!
That was fast. What do you have to say for yourselves?
I'm not going to apologize for anything or accuse anymore. I only want to state the facts.
Right now, in this frozen climate, we'd be fools to part company and go our separate ways. We have to stay together... for our survival!
Always the voice of reason, eh, Balder? But as usual, you're right. The three of us need to--
KRAK
What was that?
KRAK
KRAK
KRAK
KRAK
KRAK

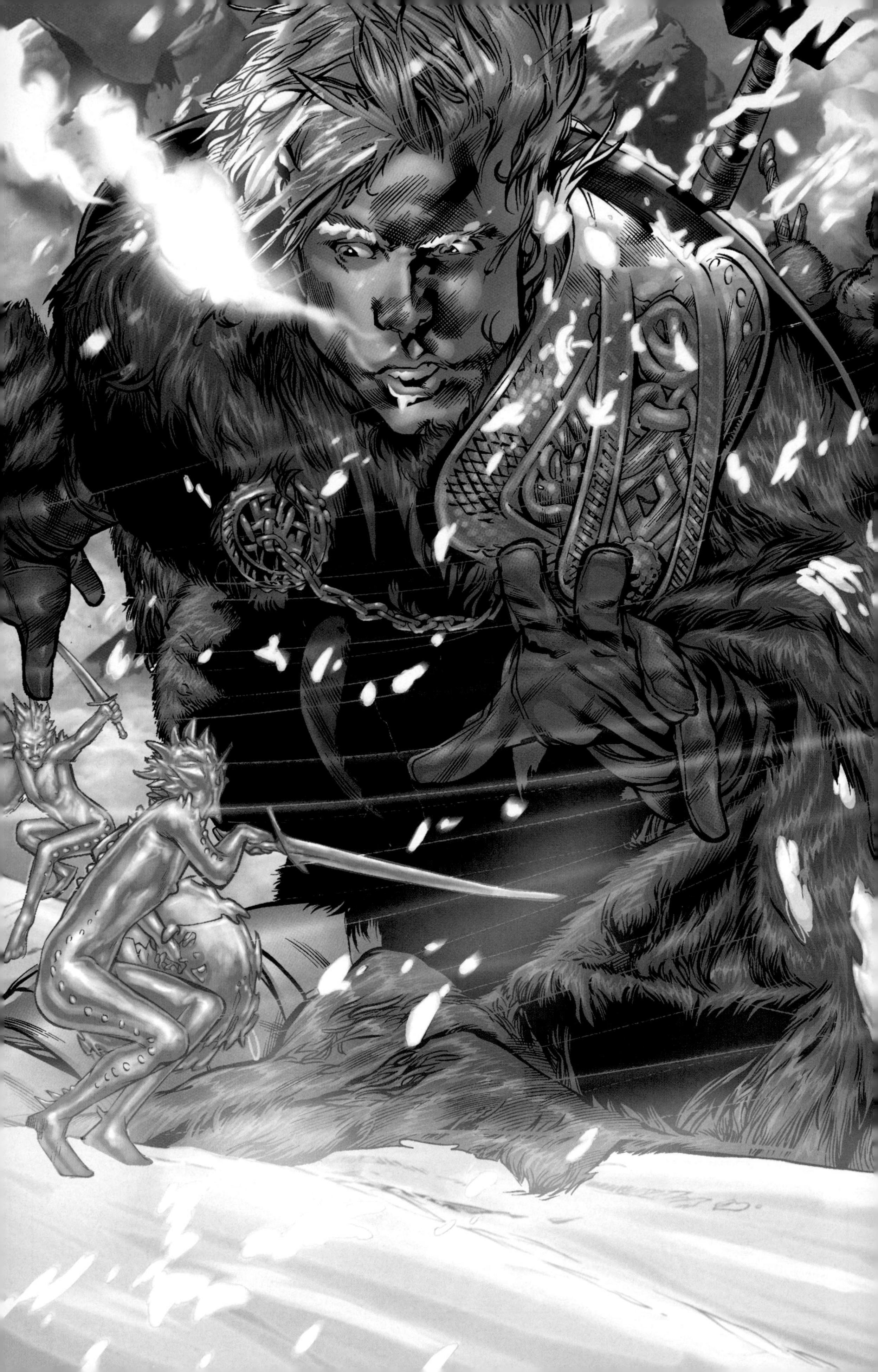

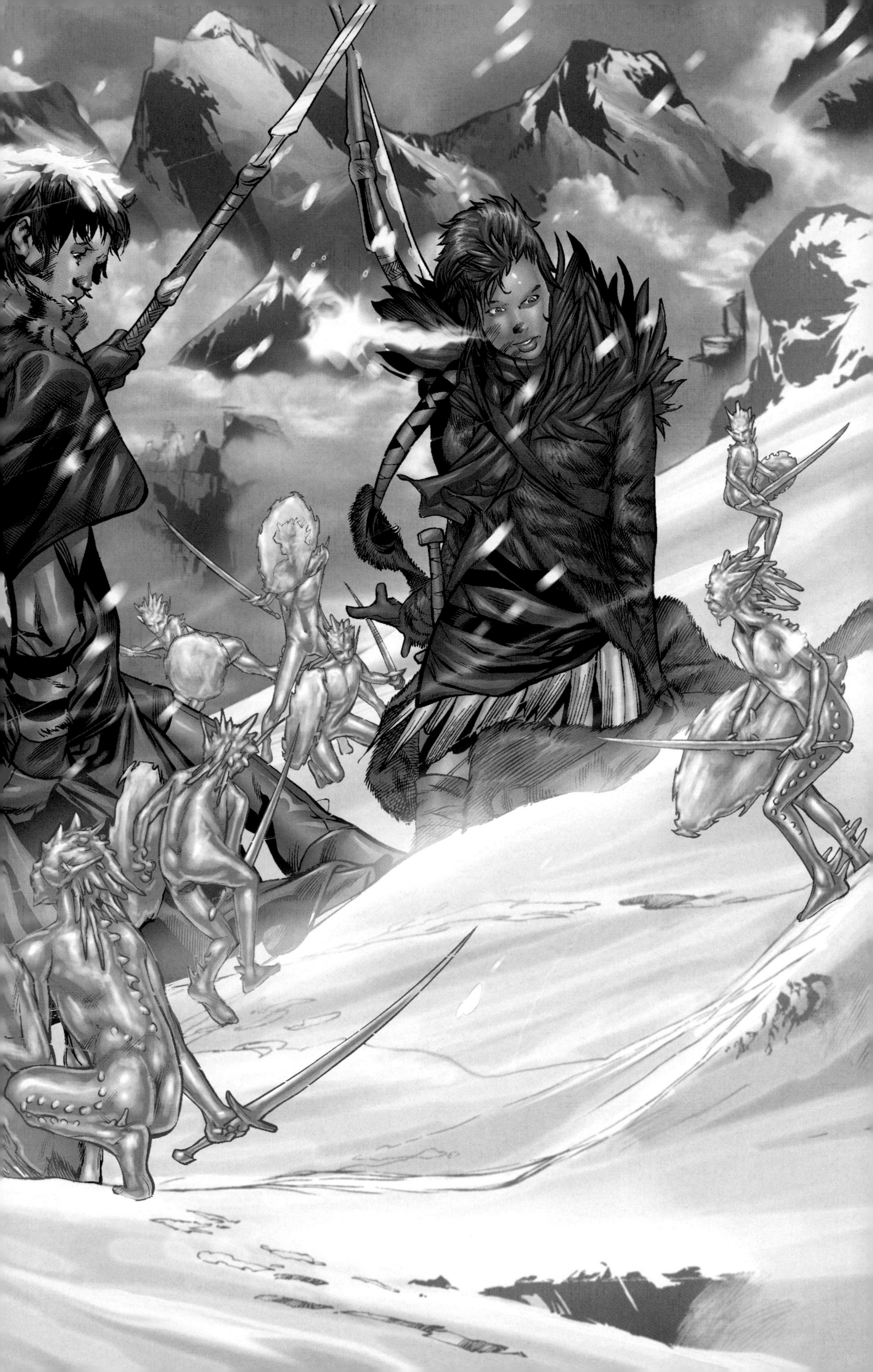

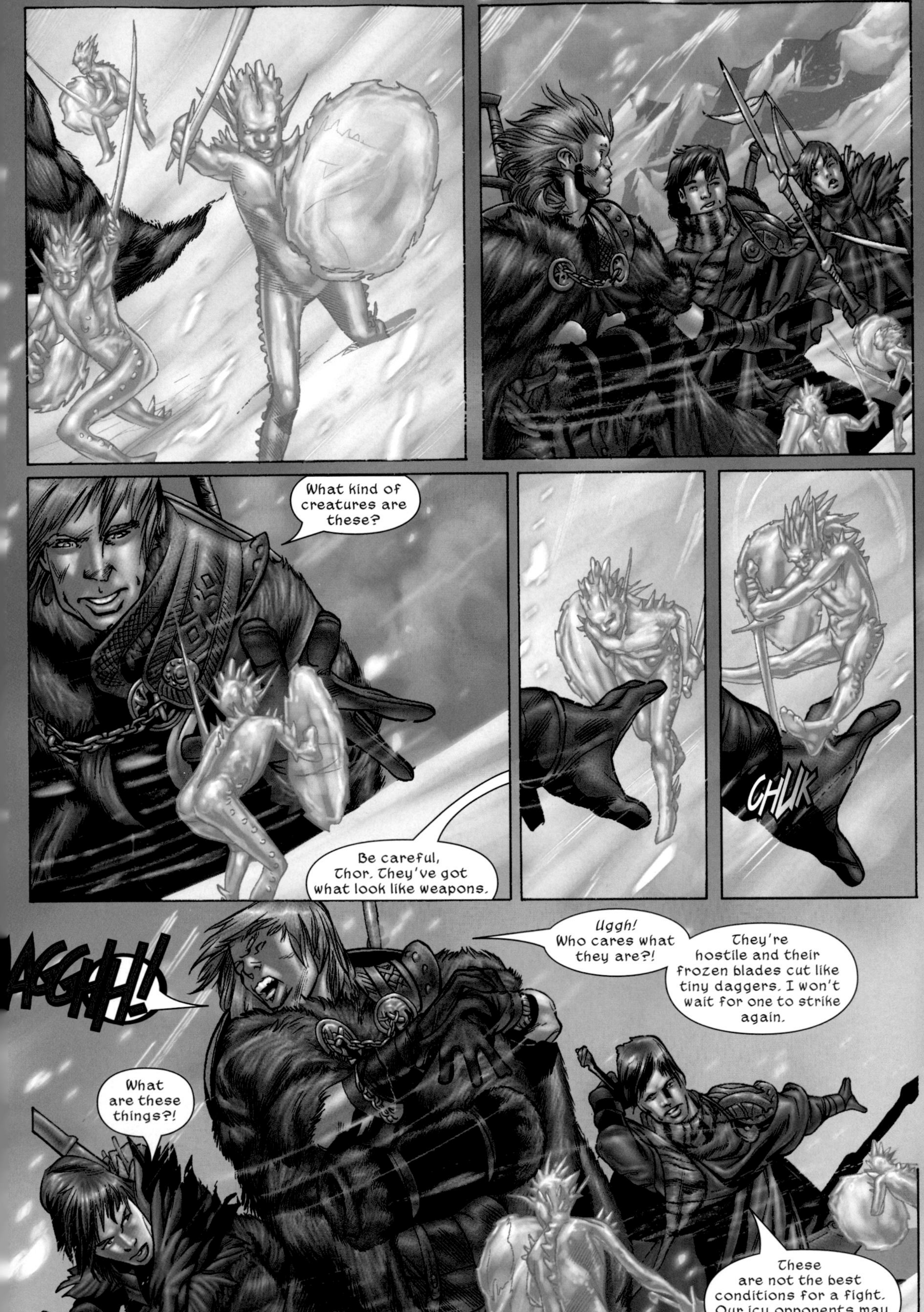
What kind of creatures are these?
Be careful, Thor. They've got what look like weapons.
CHUK
AAGGHH!
Uggh! Who cares what they are?!
They're hostile and their frozen blades cut like tiny daggers. I won't wait for one to strike again.
What are these things?!
These are not the best conditions for a fight. Our icy opponents may have the advantage here.

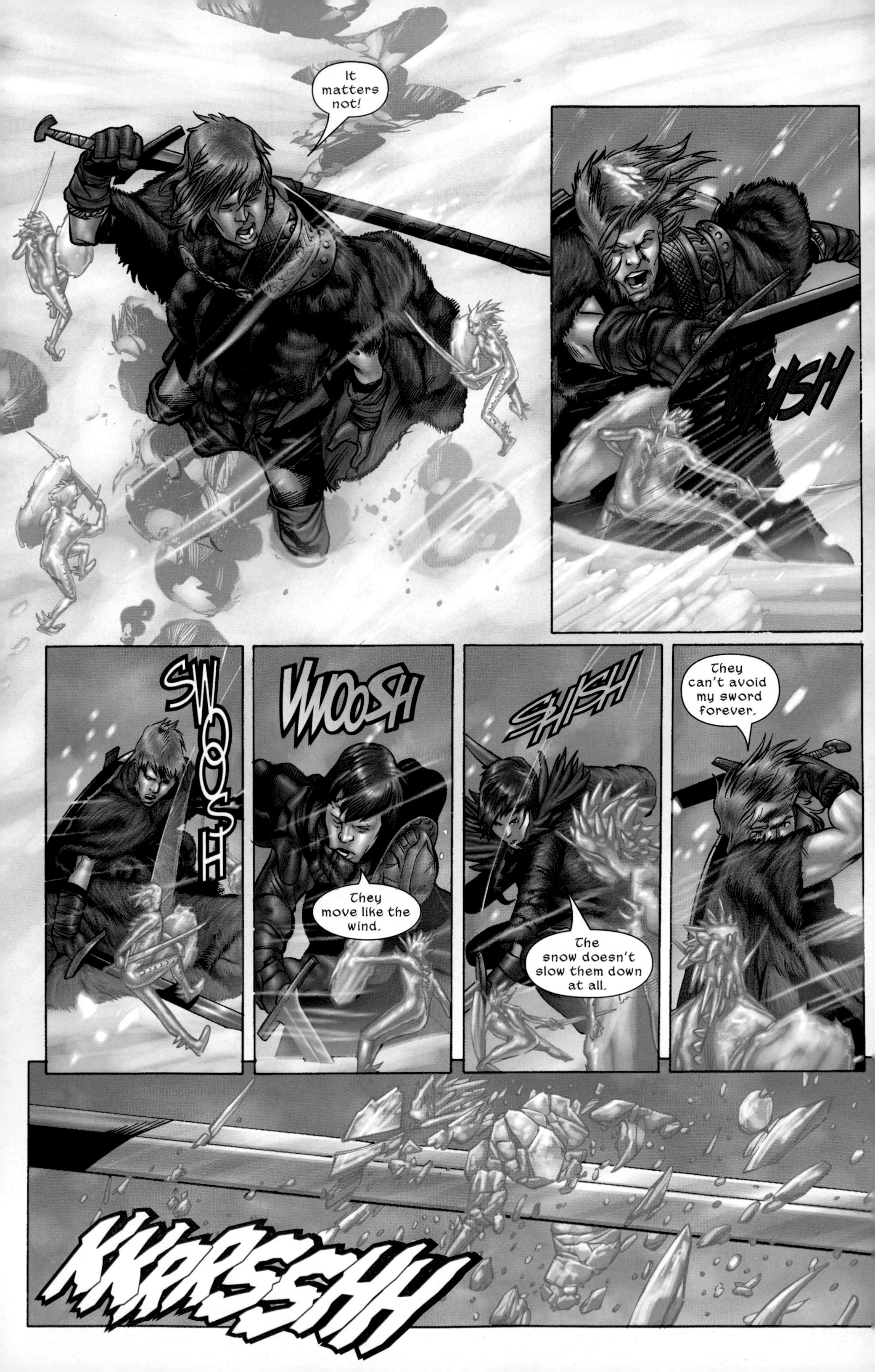

It matters not!
WHSH
SWOOSH
VVVOOSH
They move like the wind.
SHISH
The snow doesn't slow them down at all.
They can't avoid my sword forever.
KKRSSHH

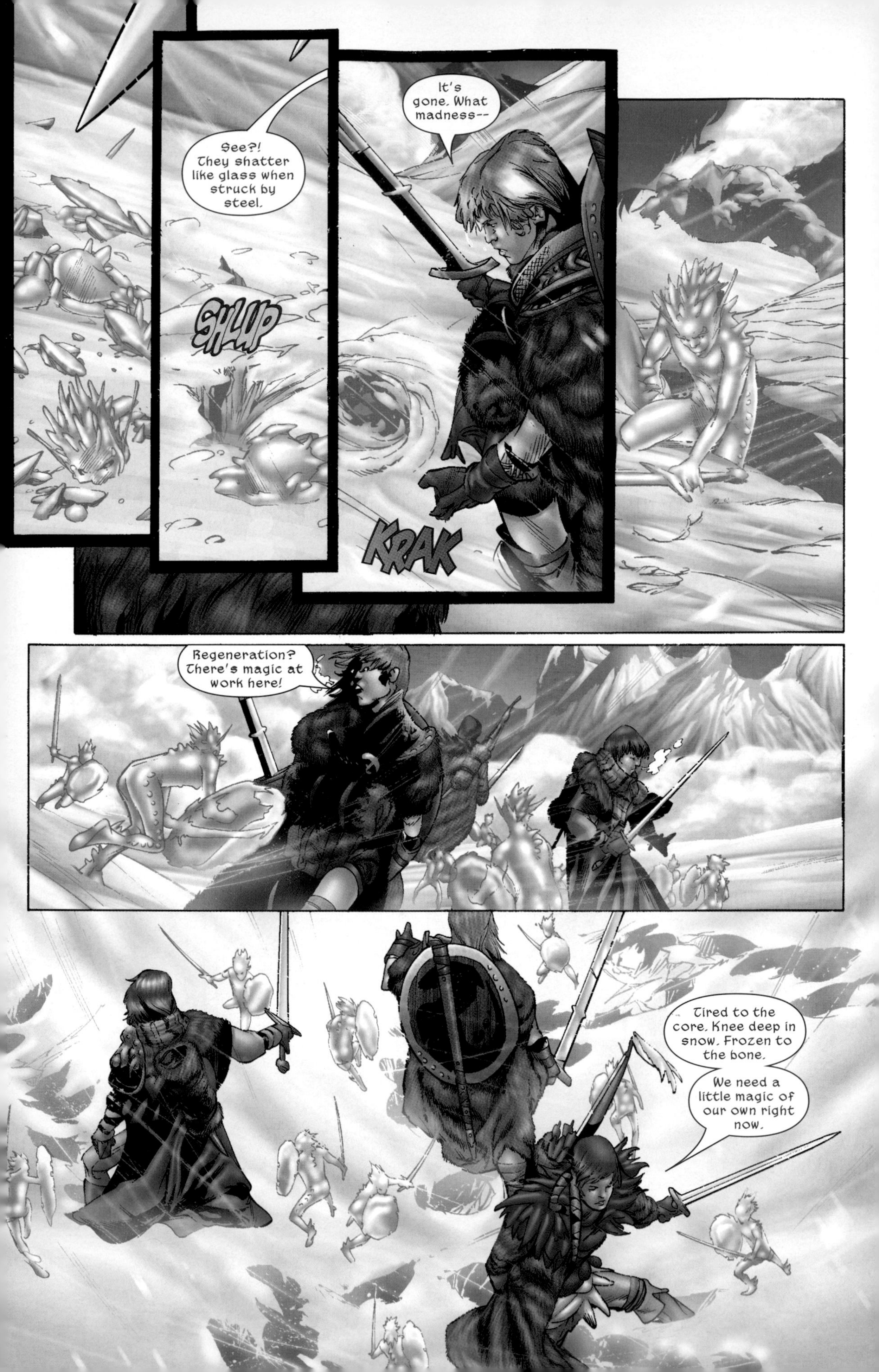
See?! They shatter like glass when struck by steel.
SHLUP
It's gone. What madness--
KRAK
Regeneration? There's magic at work here!
Tired to the core. Knee deep in snow. Frozen to the bone.
We need a little magic of our own right now.

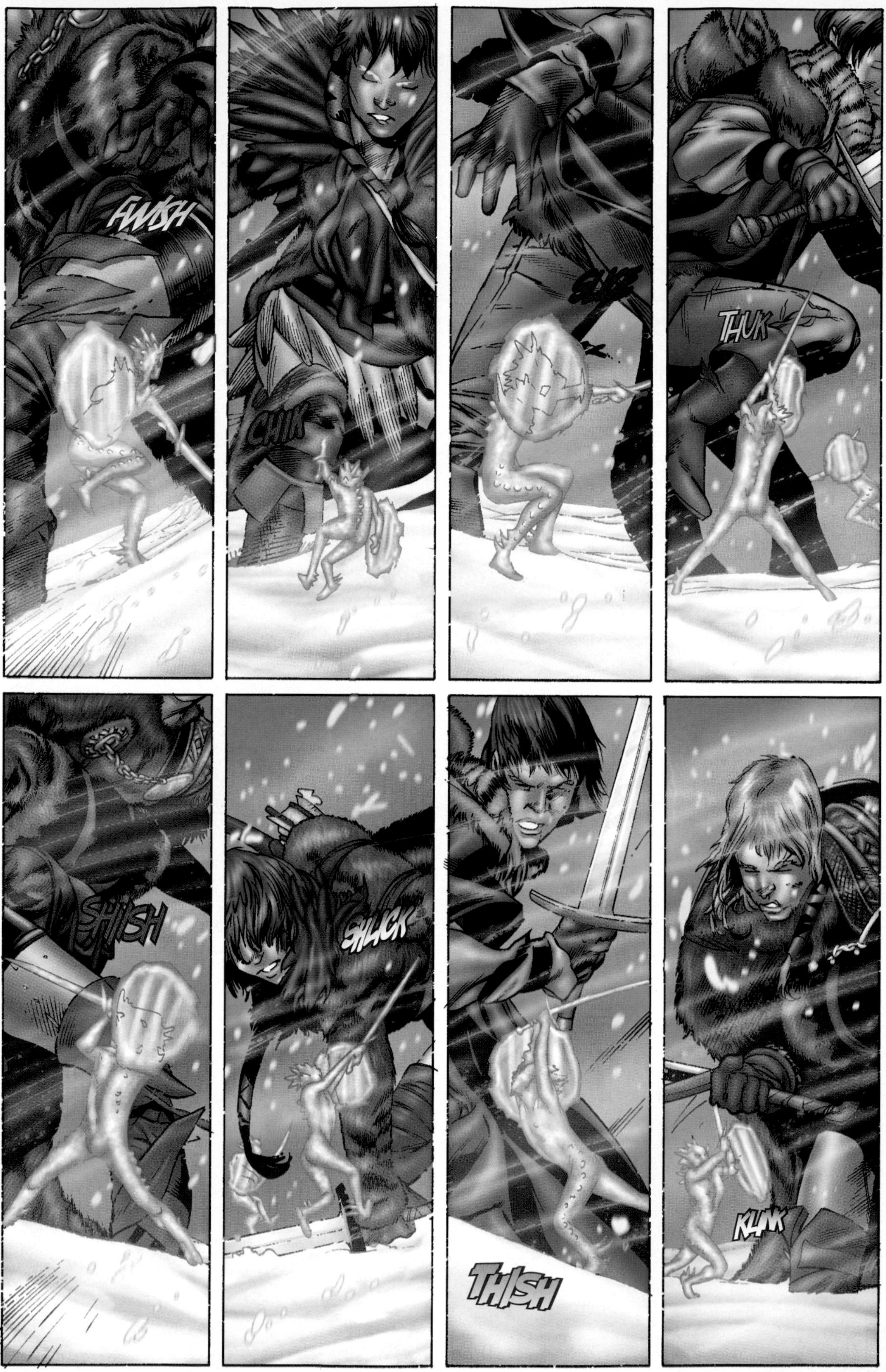
FWISH
CHIK
THUK
SHISH
SHLICK
THISH
KLINK

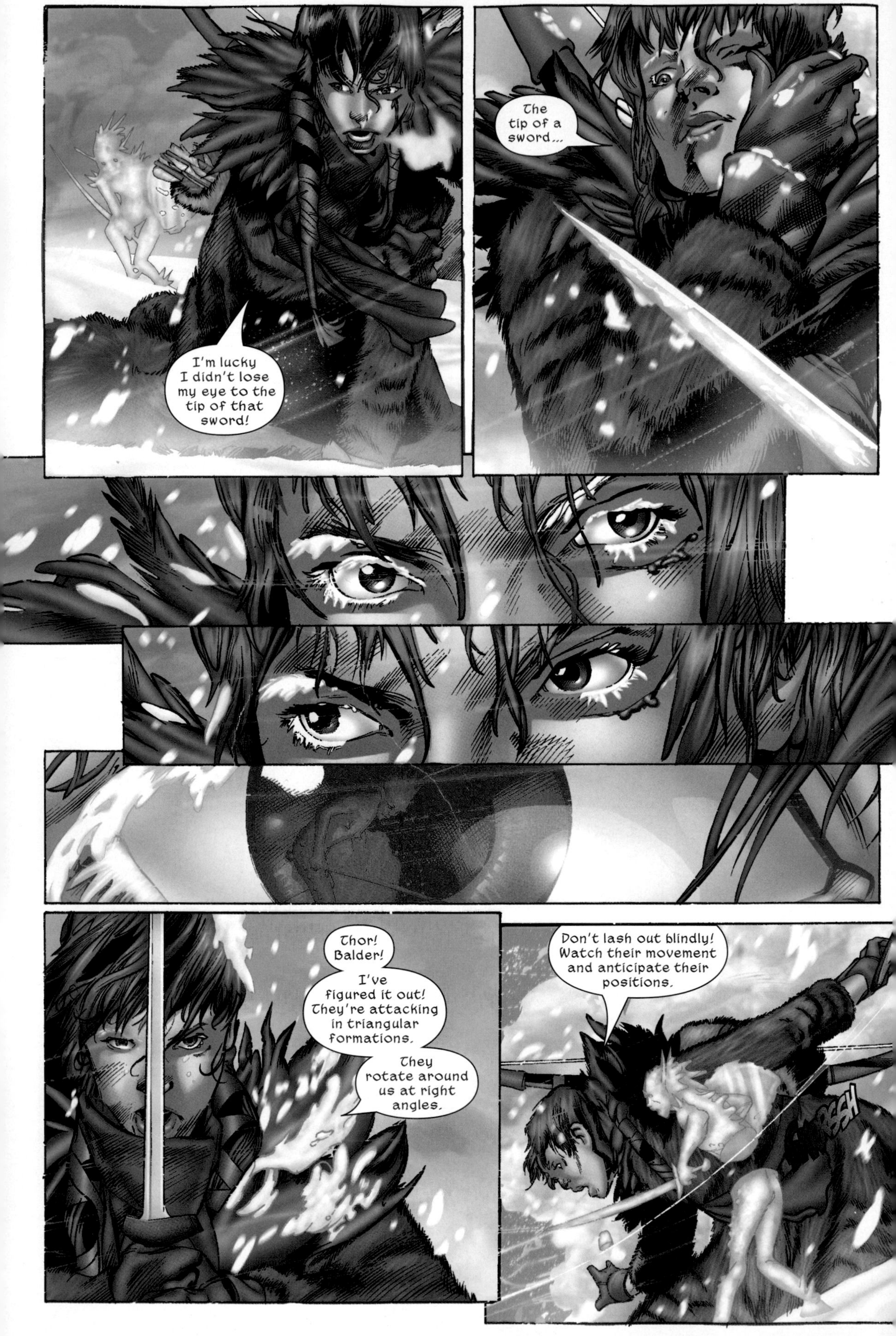
I'm lucky I didn't lose my eye to the tip of that sword!
The tip of a sword...
Thor! Balder!
I've figured it out! They're attacking in triangular formations.
They rotate around us at right angles.
Don't lash out blindly! Watch their movement and anticipate their positions.

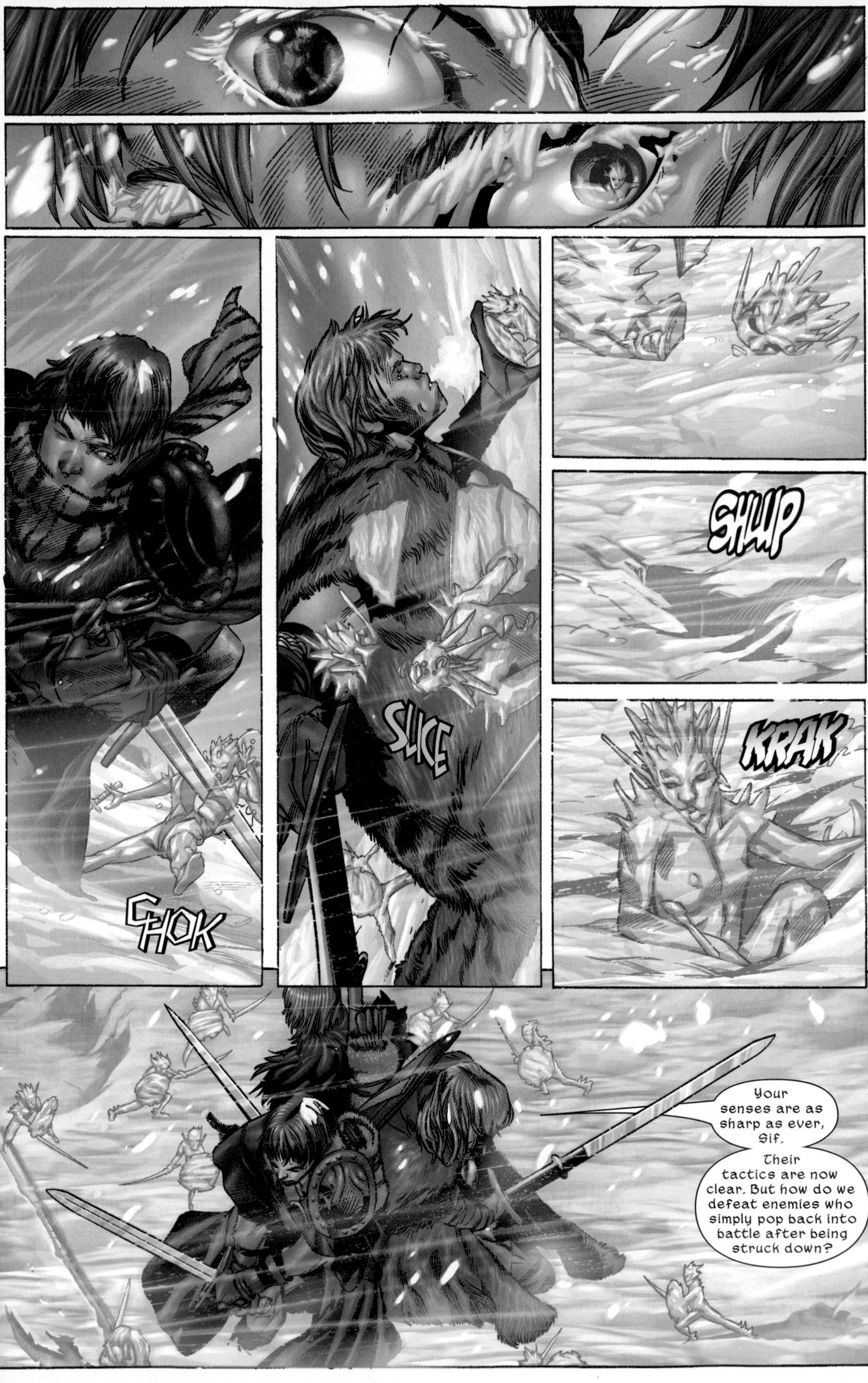
CHOK
SLICE
SHUP
KRAK
Your senses are as sharp as ever, Sif.
Their tactics are now clear. But how do we defeat enemies who simply pop back into battle after being struck down?

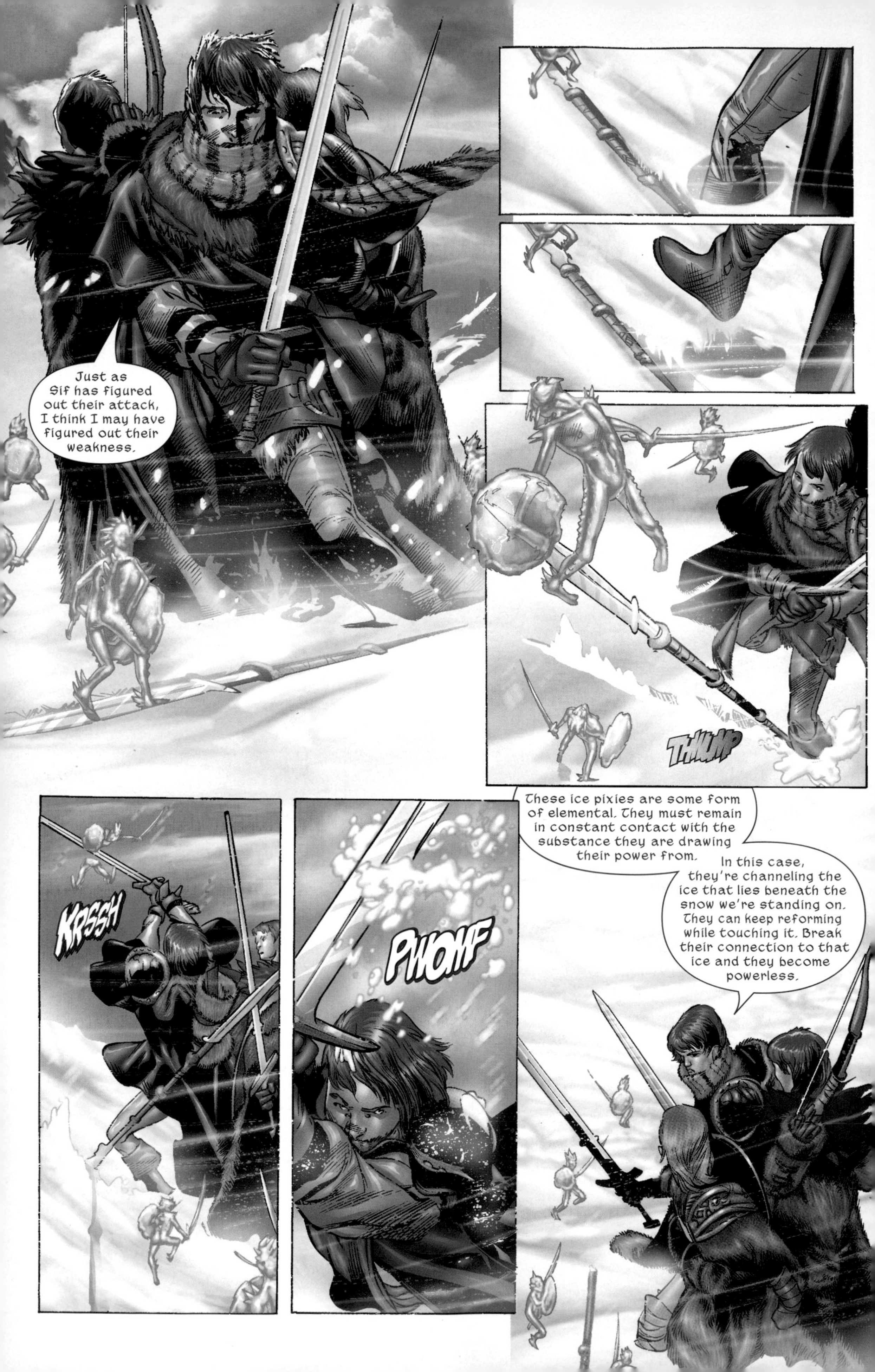
Just as Sif has figured out their attack, I think I may have figured out their weakness.
THWUMP
These ice pixies are some form of elemental. They must remain in constant contact with the substance they are drawing their power from.
In this case, they're channeling the ice that lies beneath the snow we're standing on. They can keep reforming while touching it. Break their connection to that ice and they become powerless.
KRSSH
PWOMF

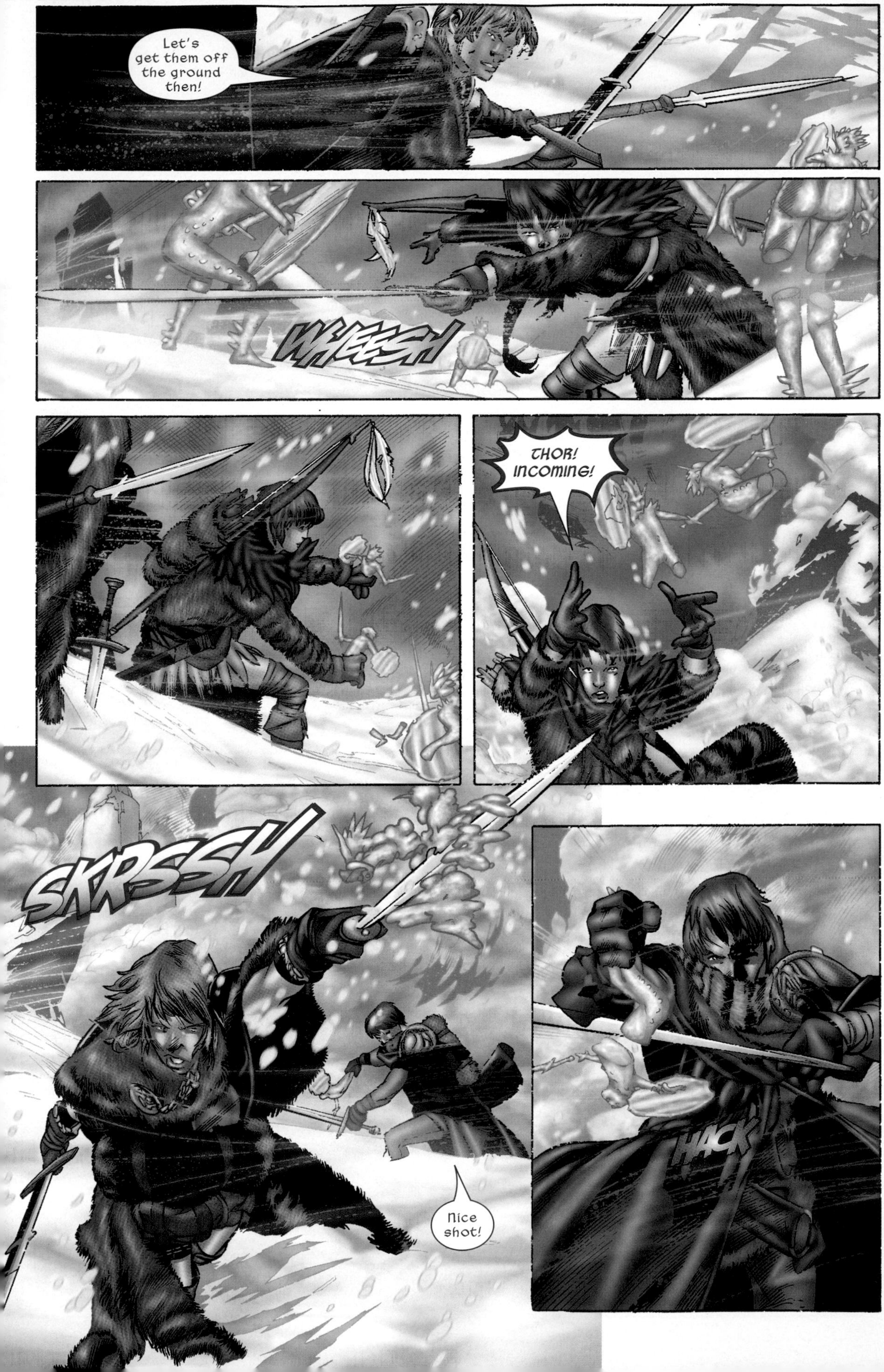
Let's get them off the ground then!
WHEESH
THOR! INCOMING!
SKRSSH
Nice shot!
HACK

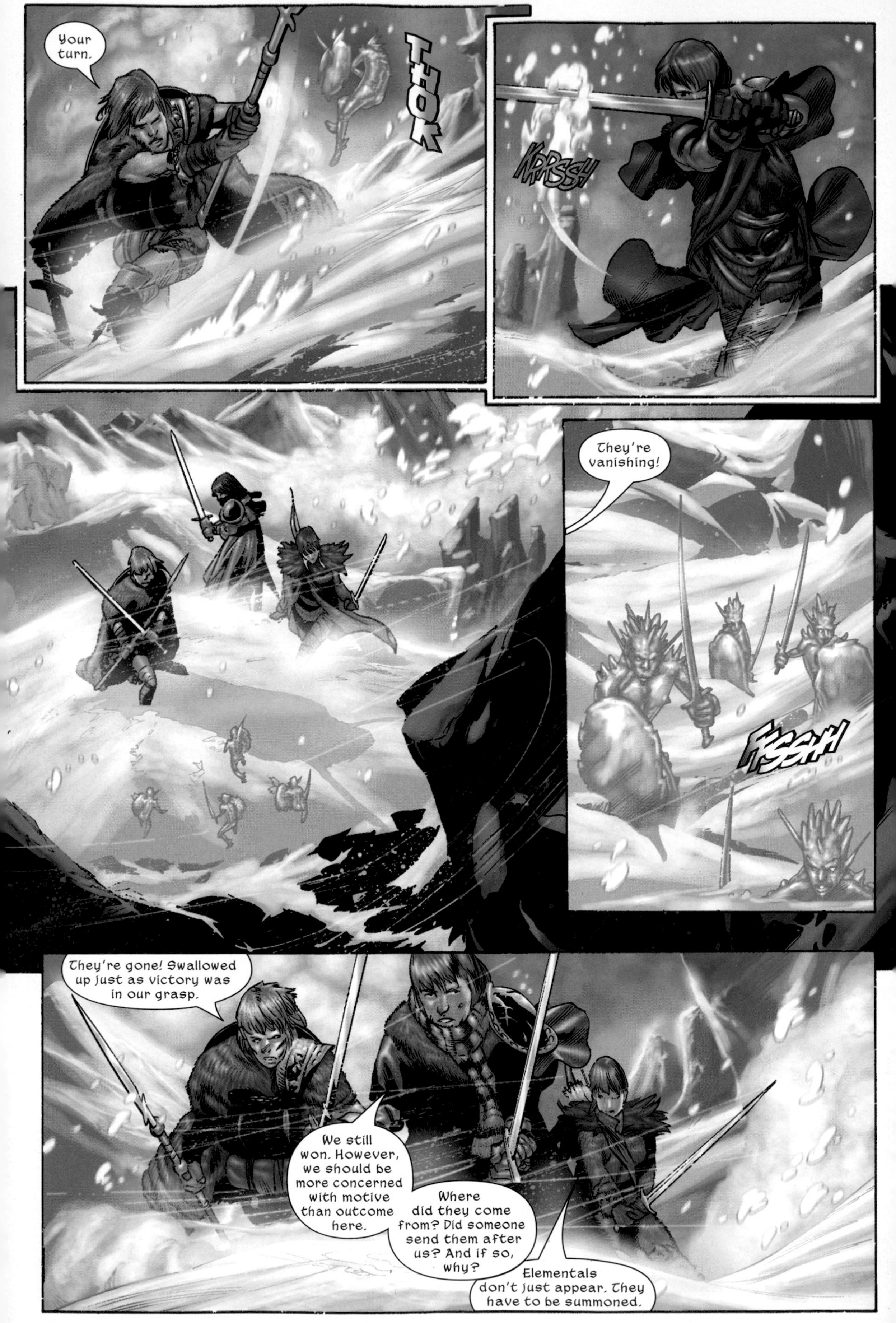
Your turn.
THOK
KRRSSH
They're vanishing!
FSSHH
They're gone! Swallowed up just as victory was in our grasp.
We still won. However, we should be more concerned with motive than outcome here.
Where did they come from? Did someone send them after us? And if so, why?
Elementals don't just appear. They have to be summoned.

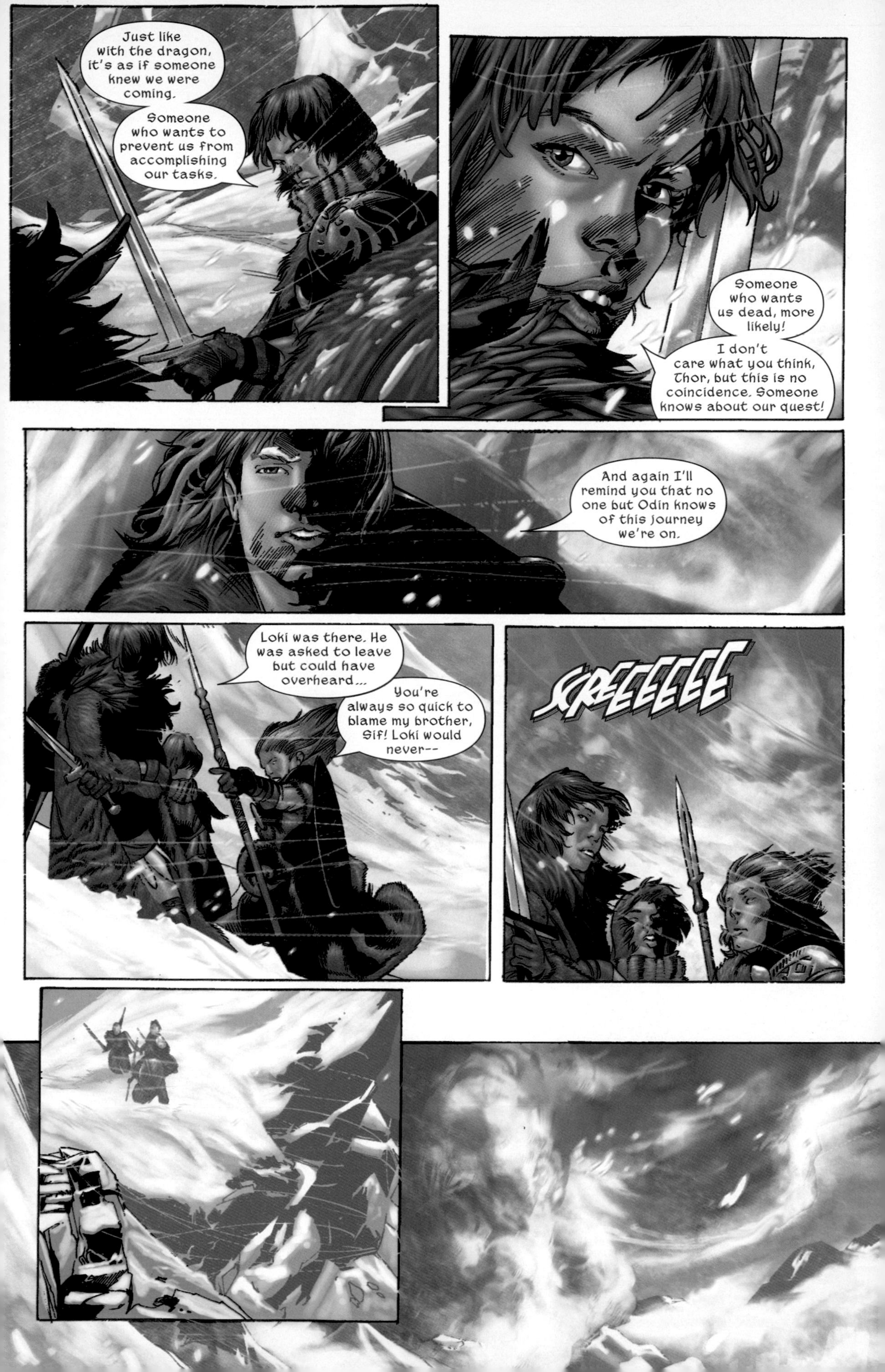
Just like with the dragon, it's as if someone knew we were coming.
Someone who wants to prevent us from accomplishing our tasks.
Someone who wants us dead, more likely!
I don't care what you think, Thor, but this is no coincidence. Someone knows about our quest!
And again I'll remind you that no one but Odin knows of this journey we're on.
Loki was there. He was asked to leave but could have overheard...
You're always so quick to blame my brother, Sif! Loki would never--
SCREEEEEEE

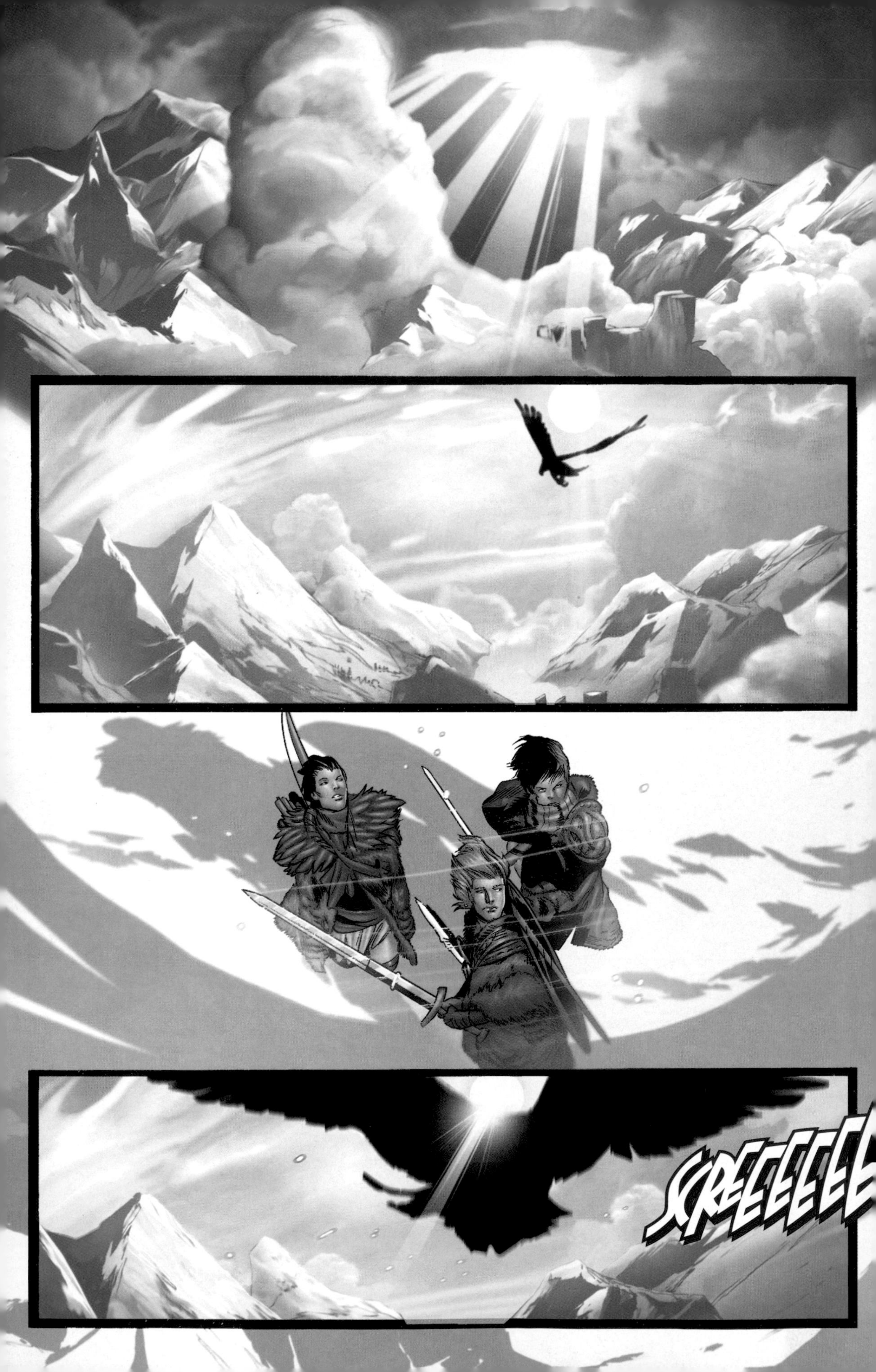
SCREEEEEE

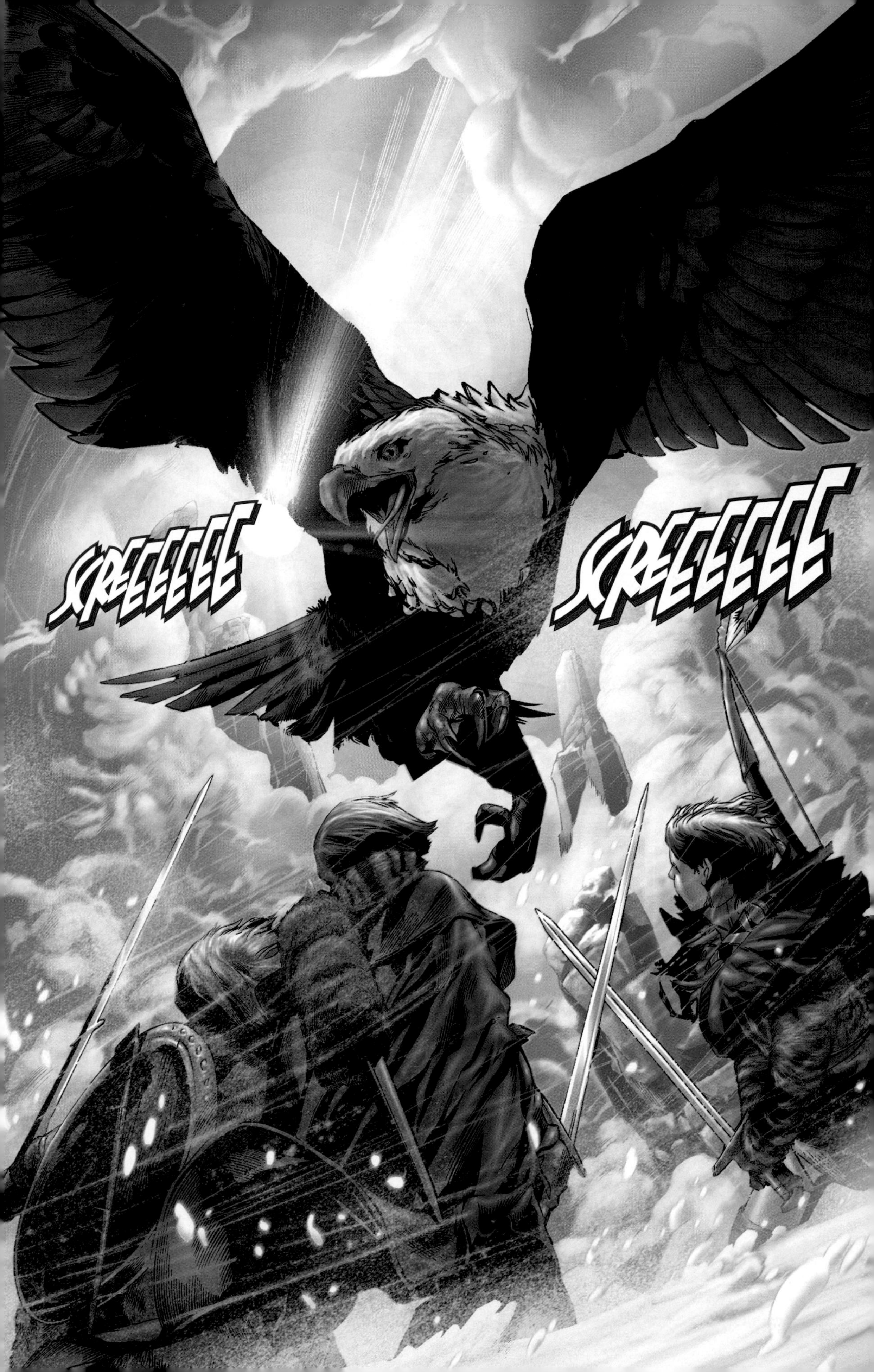
SCREEEEE
SCREEEEEEE

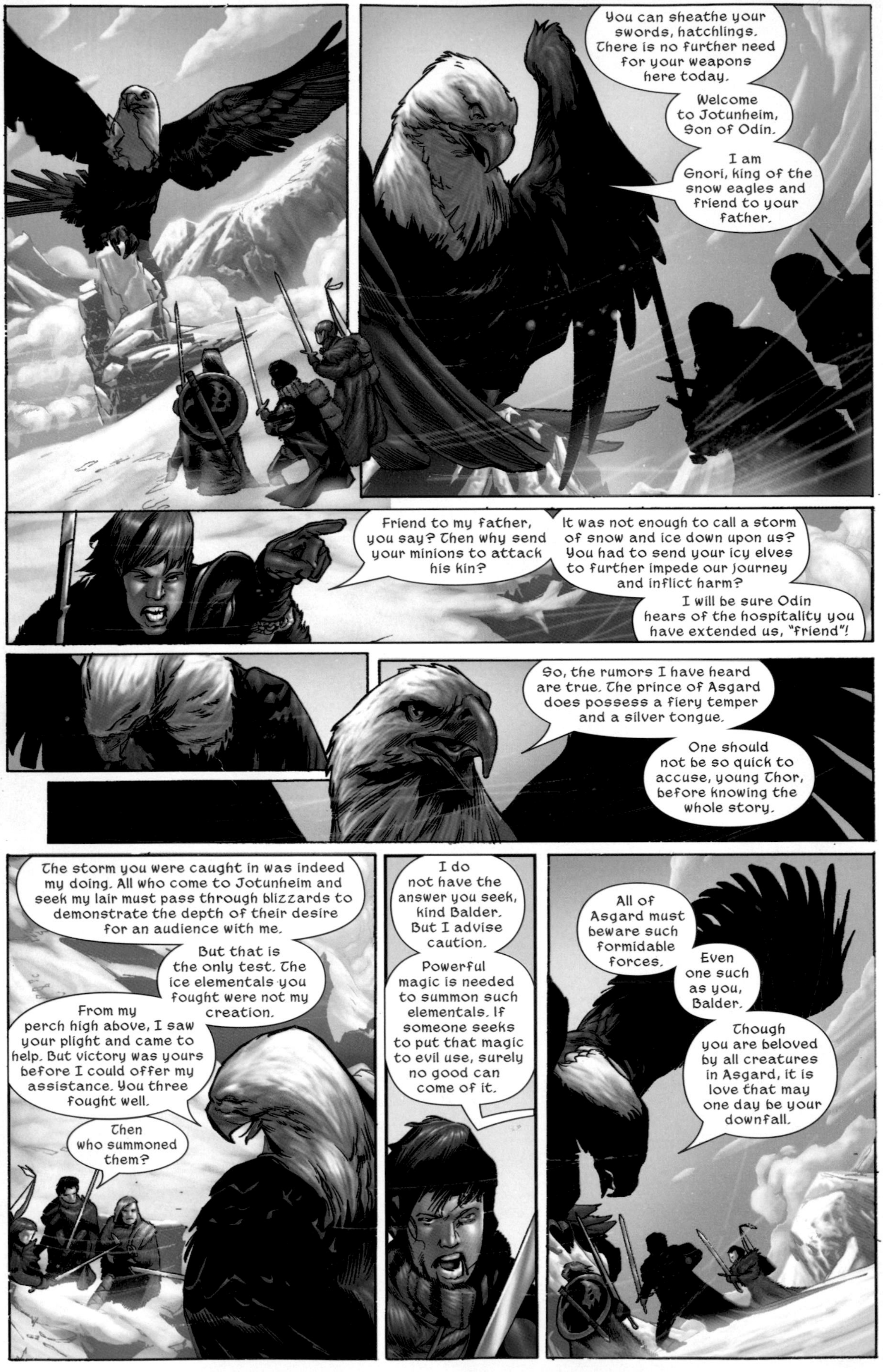
You can sheathe your swords, hatchlings. There is no further need for your weapons here today.
Welcome to Jotunheim, Son of Odin.
I am Gnori, king of the snow eagles and friend to your father.
Friend to my father, you say? Then why send your minions to attack his kin?
It was not enough to call a storm of snow and ice down upon us? You had to send your icy elves to further impede our journey and inflict harm?
I will be sure Odin hears of the hospitality you have extended us, "friend"!
So, the rumors I have heard are true. The prince of Asgard does possess a fiery temper and a silver tongue.
One should not be so quick to accuse, young Thor, before knowing the whole story.
The storm you were caught in was indeed my doing. All who come to Jotunheim and seek my lair must pass through blizzards to demonstrate the depth of their desire for an audience with me.
But that is the only test. The ice elementals you fought were not my creation.
From my perch high above, I saw your plight and came to help. But victory was yours before I could offer my assistance. You three fought well.
Then who summoned them?
I do not have the answer you seek, kind Balder. But I advise caution.
Powerful magic is needed to summon such elementals. If someone seeks to put that magic to evil use, surely no good can come of it.
All of Asgard must beware such formidable forces.
Even one such as you, Balder.
Though you are beloved by all creatures in Asgard, it is love that may one day be your downfall.

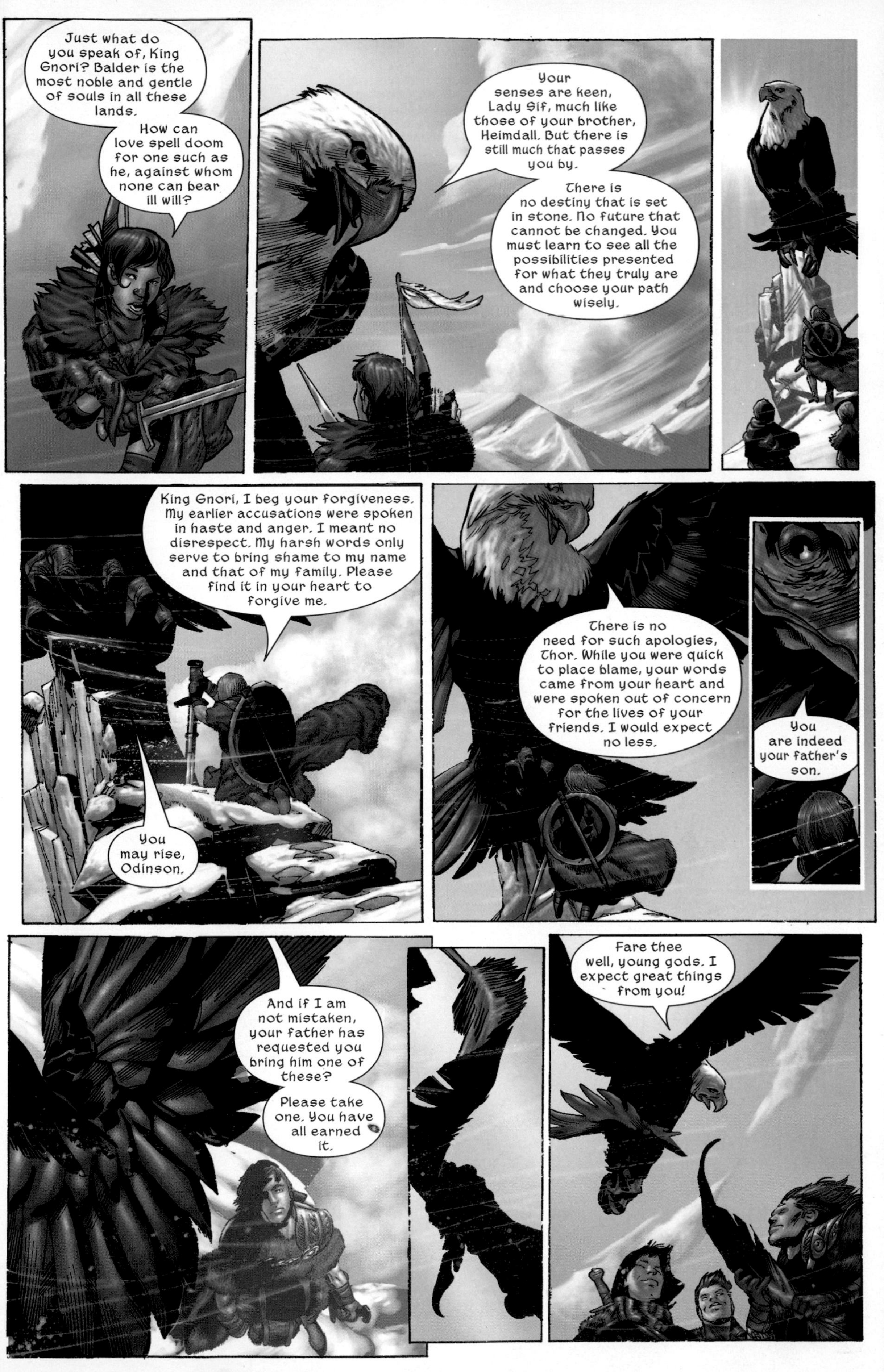
Just what do you speak of, King Gnori? Balder is the most noble and gentle of souls in all these lands.
How can love spell doom for one such as he, against whom none can bear ill will?
Your senses are keen, Lady Sif, much like those of your brother, Heimdall. But there is still much that passes you by.
There is no destiny that is set in stone. No future that cannot be changed. You must learn to see all the possibilities presented for what they truly are and choose your path wisely.
King Gnori, I beg your forgiveness. My earlier accusations were spoken in haste and anger. I meant no disrespect. My harsh words only serve to bring shame to my name and that of my family. Please find it in your heart to forgive me.
You may rise, Odinson.
There is no need for such apologies, Thor. While you were quick to place blame, your words came from your heart and were spoken out of concern for the lives of your friends. I would expect no less.
You are indeed your father's son.
And if I am not mistaken, your father has requested you bring him one of these?
Please take one. You have all earned it.
Fare thee well, young gods. I expect great things from you!

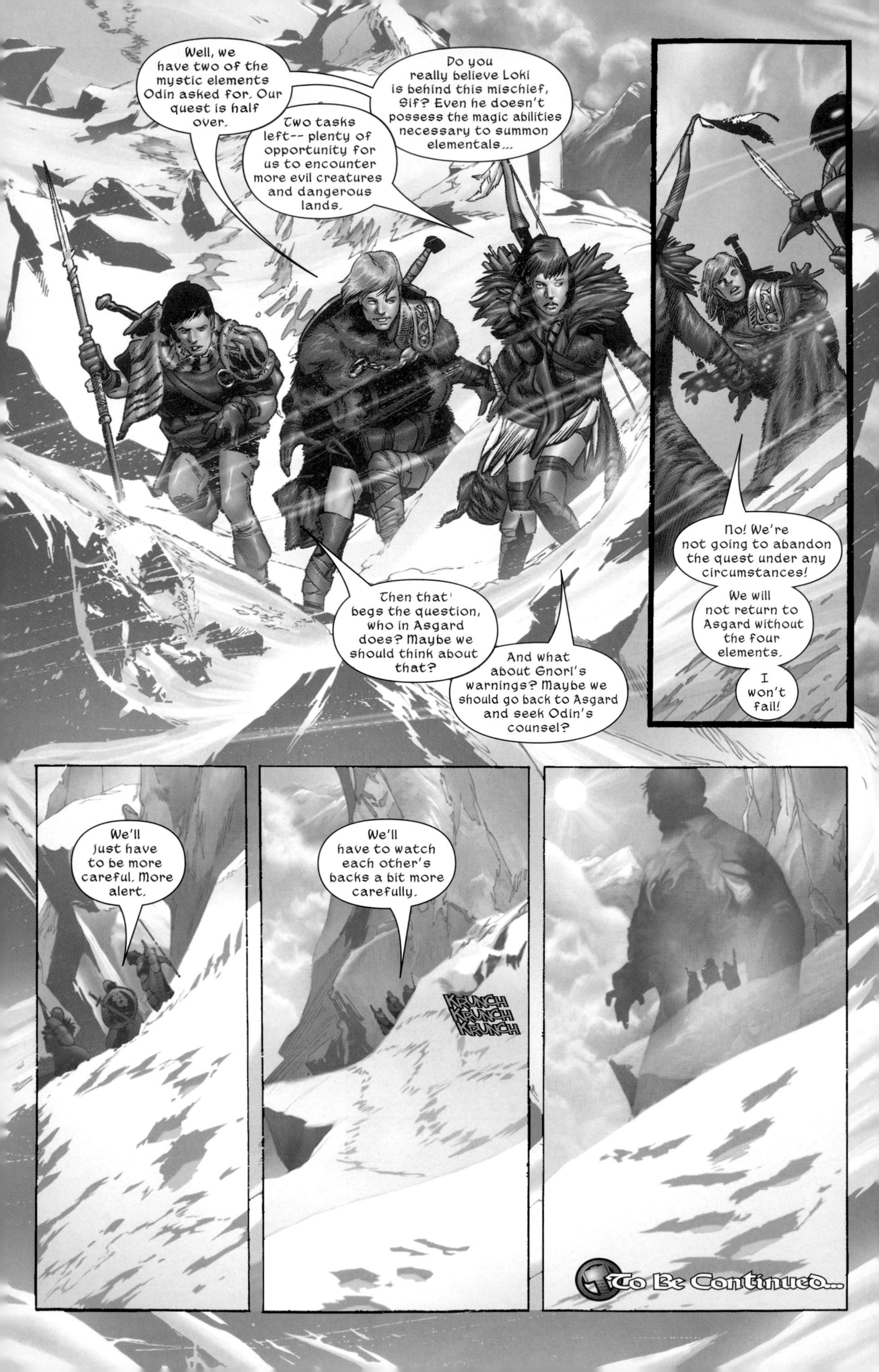
Well, we have two of the mystic elements Odin asked for. Our quest is half over.
Two tasks left-- plenty of opportunity for us to encounter more evil creatures and dangerous lands.
Do you really believe Loki is behind this mischief, Sif? Even he doesn't possess the magic abilities necessary to summon elementals...
Then that begs the question, who in Asgard does? Maybe we should think about that?
And what about Gnorl's warnings? Maybe we should go back to Asgard and seek Odin's counsel?
No! We're not going to abandon the quest under any circumstances!
We will not return to Asgard without the four elements.
I won't fail!
We'll just have to be more careful. More alert.
We'll have to watch each other's backs a bit more carefully.
KRUNCH KRUNCH KRUNCH
To Be Continued...